ZIGBY ™

AND THE ANT INVADERS

BRIAN PATERSON

Collins

An imprint of HarperCollinsPublishers

Have you read all the books about Zigby?

Zigby Camps Out
Zigby Hunts for Treasure
Zigby and the Ant Invaders
Zigby Dives In

For William, Charles and Henry

First published in Great Britain by HarperCollins Publishers Ltd in 2003

1 3 5 7 9 10 8 6 4 2

ISBN: 0-00-713166-6

Text copyright © Alan MacDonald, Brian and Cynthia Paterson and HarperCollins Publishers Ltd 2003
Illustrations copyright © Brian Paterson 2003

Text by Alan MacDonald

ZIGBY™ and the Zigby character logo are trademarks of HarperCollins Publishers Ltd.

The authors and illustrator assert the moral right to
be identified as the authors and illustrator of the work.
A CIP catalogue record for this title is available from the British Library.

The HarperCollins website address is: www.fireandwater.com

Printed and bound in Belgium by Proost

Follow the winding stream to the
edge of the jungly forest and meet...

ZIGBY THE ZEBRA
OF MUDWATER CREEK.

Zigby the Zebra loves being outdoors, getting up
to mischief with his good friends, Bertie and McMeer.
There are always exciting new places to explore
and wonderful adventures waiting to happen
but sometimes he can't help trotting
straight into trouble!

Meet his friend, the African guinea fowl, Bertie Bird.
He's easily scared and thinks his friends are far too
naughty...but he'd hate to miss the fun, even if it does
mean getting dirty feathers!

McMeer is the cheeky little meerkat who
loves showing off and playing tricks. His practical
jokes sometimes cause all sorts of problems,
but he always knows how to have fun!

IT WAS NIGHT TIME IN MUDWATER CREEK.
Outside Zigby's tree house it had been raining hard.
Inside, strange noises were keeping him awake.
Zigby shone his torch all round the room.
"Who's there?" he asked in a small voice.
No one answered. Zigby lay down
again and tried to sleep.

In the morning, Zigby sat up with surprise.
There was an ant asleep on his pillow!
The ant yawned and stretched.
"Who are you?" asked Zigby, scratching.
"I'm Tiny," said the ant. "What's for breakfast?"

"Where do you live?" asked Zigby, over breakfast.
Tiny looked forlorn.
"Our ant hill was swept away in the rain," he said.
"My family sent me on ahead to find a new home."
"Never mind," said Zigby. "You could stay here
for a while. I've got plenty of room."
"Great!" said Tiny.
"When's lunch?"

While Tiny inspected the fridge, Zigby went to find his friends, Bertie Bird and McMeer. He told them about his visitor.

"He's an ant," explained Zigby.

"That's funny," said Bertie. "I've just seen lots of ants. Come and see!"

Over the hill they found a long line of ants trooping through the grass.

"I wonder where they're all going?" said Zigby.

"Let's follow and see," suggested Bertie.

They followed the ants under the shadow of some giant leaves, past a pack of surprised monkeys and across the muddy creek...

...until they reached a house.
"But that's *my* house!" exclaimed Zigby.
"Hello!" said Tiny. "Meet my family.
You said they could stay!"

Tiny's big family soon made themselves at home.
They ate everything in Zigby's cupboards.
They used his bathtub as a slide. And they
turned up in the most surprising places.
"This is great," said Tiny at supper.
"Just you, me and my family."
"Perfect," said Zigby, gloomily.
"What's for afters?"
asked Tiny.

Zigby took Bertie and McMeer outside.
"What am I going to do?" he moaned. "Those ants eat everything and they're driving me *crazy!*"

"Leave it to me," said McMeer. "I know how to get rid of them."

McMeer called the ants together.

"We're going to play a game," he announced.

"Great!" said Tiny. "I love games!"

"Everyone follow me!" said McMeer, leading them out of the house.

They walked and walked until
they were deep in the forest.
"This is the place," said McMeer.
"We're going to play hide and seek.
You ants count to ten then
come and look for us."

The ants covered their eyes while Zigby,
Bertie and McMeer went to hide.
"How is this going to get rid of
them?" whispered Zigby.
"You'll see," said McMeer.
"Found you!" shouted
Tiny, excitedly.

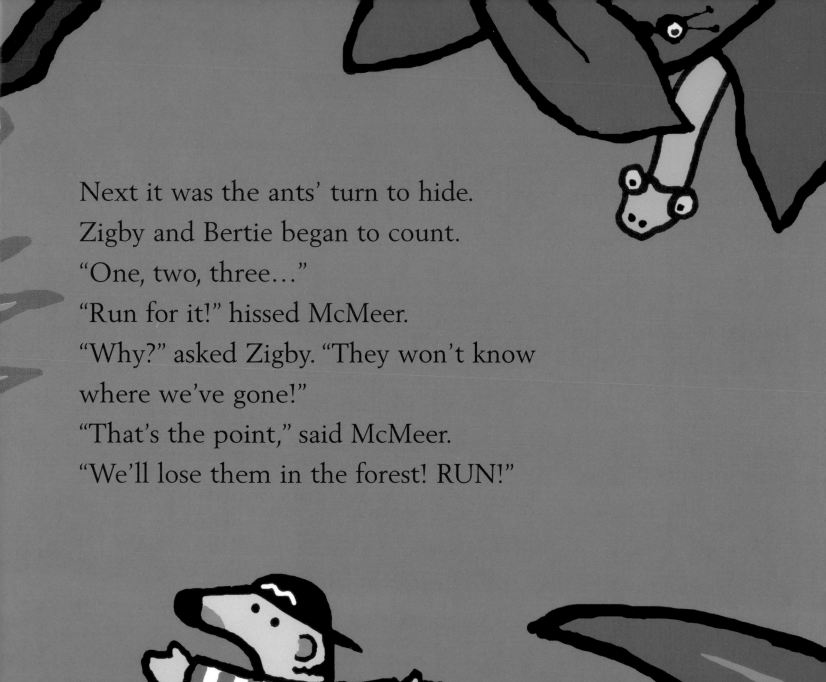

Next it was the ants' turn to hide.
Zigby and Bertie began to count.
"One, two, three…"
"Run for it!" hissed McMeer.
"Why?" asked Zigby. "They won't know
where we've gone!"
"That's the point," said McMeer.
"We'll lose them in the forest! RUN!"

The three friends ran off into the bushes. They didn't stop running until they reached Zigby's tree house.

"Have we lost them?" panted Bertie.

"I think so," said Zigby.

"Don't worry," said McMeer, confidently. "We won't be seeing those ants again!"

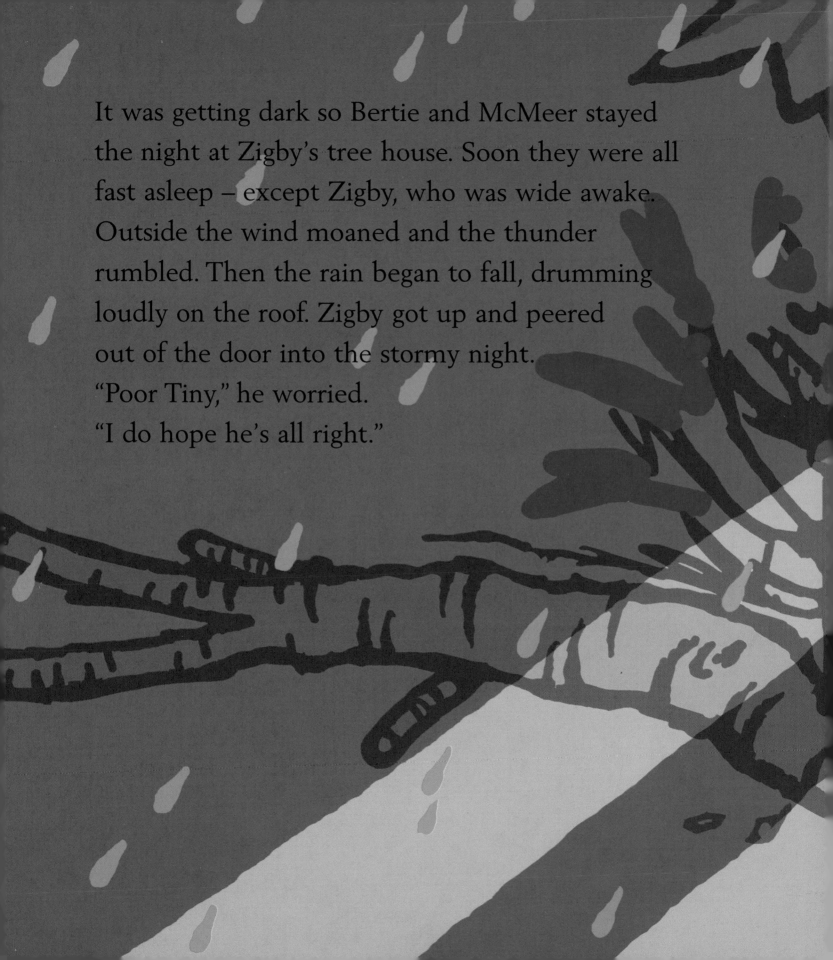

It was getting dark so Bertie and McMeer stayed
the night at Zigby's tree house. Soon they were all
fast asleep – except Zigby, who was wide awake.
Outside the wind moaned and the thunder
rumbled. Then the rain began to fall, drumming
loudly on the roof. Zigby got up and peered
out of the door into the stormy night.
"Poor Tiny," he worried.
"I do hope he's all right."

In the morning the storm had passed
and the sun was shining.
"Come on!" said Zigby, bounding out of bed.
"We've got to find them!"
"Find who?" asked McMeer, sleepily.
"The ants, of course! They could have
been swept away in the storm!"

They searched the forest calling Tiny's name.
They looked under rocks, peered into logs and poked
around in muddy puddles. There was no sign of the ants.
"It's all my fault!" groaned Zigby. "We should never have
run off and left them."

Bertie pointed. "Look! It's Tiny!"
"Tiny!" said Zigby. "You're all right!
Didn't you get caught in the storm?"
"No," said Tiny. "We found a great place to stay.
Come and see!"

They followed Tiny to a house set in a muddy hillside.
"But that's...that's my house!" wailed McMeer.
"You can't stay there!"
"Wait a minute," said Zigby. "This mud might be
the answer. Come with me..."

It was muddy work but Tiny was delighted.
"Our own tree house! Thanks, Zigby," he said.
"Now we're neighbours, we can drop in for tea!"